BILLY the GOAT
Big Breakfast

Jez
Alborough

To Adele

 *Billy's Breakfast Song* can be heard
and downloaded, along with the sheet
music, from **jezalborough.com/billythegoat**

BILLY THE GOAT'S BIG BREAKFAST
A RED FOX BOOK
978 1 782 95135 3

First published in Great Britain by Doubleday, an imprint of Random House Children's Publishers UK
A Random House Group Company

Doubleday edition published 2013
This edition published 2014

1 3 5 7 9 10 8 6 4 2
Copyright © Jez Alborough, 2013
Billy's Breakfast Song © Jez Alborough, 2013

With thanks to Philippa and Dave for help with the musical notation.

RANDOM HOUSE CHILDREN'S PUBLISHERS UK
61–63 Uxbridge Road, London W5 5SA

www.**randomhousechildrens**.co.uk
www.**randomhouse**.co.uk

Addresses for companies within The Random House Group Limited can be found at:
www.randomhouse.co.uk/offices.htm

THE RANDOM HOUSE GROUP Limited Reg. No. 954009

A CIP catalogue record for this book is available from the British Library.

Printed in China

Nat the Cat made a breakfast to share
with her friends Billy Goat and Hugo Hare.
She was going to make a breakfast treat,
with some lovely homemade bread to eat.

Nat mixed up water, flour and stuff
until it was stretchy and springy enough,

then left it to rise in a small gooey ball –
that's when the doorbell rang in the hall.

'Hi, Billy,' said Nat, 'come in, take a seat.'
'I'm ever so hungry,' said Billy, 'let's eat!'

He ran to the kitchen and down he sat.
'We can't start breakfast yet,' cried Nat.

'You've come too early – the food isn't made,
the juice isn't juiced and the table's not laid.
And Hugo Hare won't be here until eight,
we can't start without him – you'll just have to wait.'

Billy Goat sighed and stared at the bread,
'I'm not very good at waiting,' he said.
'Why don't you lay the table?' said Nat.
'You'll have waited a lot by the time you've done that.'

So Billy brought butter, jam and three mugs,
some knives and plates and the juice in a jug.

He slowly laid out the cups, knives and plates
then ran out of things to do – except wait.

But the food made waiting harder because
his tummy kept saying how hungry he was.
The juice in the jug looked zingy and yummy,
'I want some of that,' cried Billy Goat's tummy.

Billy thought that he'd take just a couple of sips
as he lifted the jug to his slobbery lips.
He gulped and he glugged then he took a big slurp,
put down the jug, then burped a big **BURP**.

Billy's tum was still hungry, it wanted some more,
he looked round the kitchen and guess what he saw?

There, on the stove, sat the mix for the bread.
'Have a nibble on that,' his tummy said.

Billy tried to resist,
he knew that he should,
but he felt so hungry,
the bread looked so good.
He closed both his eyes
and gave up the fight,
as his mouth opened wide
and he took a big bite.

'**YUCK!**' thought Billy. 'This bread is too chewy!
It should be all crumbly, not squishy and gooey.'
Just then someone called his name from outside,
'Hi, Billy! It's Hugo – I'm here,' he cried.

Billy tried to answer, but what could he do?
His mouth was full of a big lump of goo!

He just couldn't speak, he felt such a chump,
so with one great, big **GULP**

he swallowed
the lump.

'Hello,' said Billy, as his friends bustled in,
but Nat saw beyond Billy's big, sticky grin.

The juice was all gone, to the very last drop
and the mix had a bite-sized hole in the top.

Nat turned on the oven and put in the mix,
but then she was left with a problem to fix –

now there's not enough food to get them all fed.
'I'm just popping out for a minute,' she said.

'Oh, Hugo,' said Billy, with a lump in his throat.
'I've been such a naughty, greedy goat.
I knew it was wrong and I knew it was rude,
but before you came in I ate half the food.
The horrible bread made my tummy rumble
and now it's started to gurgle and grumble.'

His tummy did something else as well –
as it mumbled and rumbled it started to swell.
Hugo could hardly believe what he saw.
It was twice the size that it had been before!

'I'm back,' cried Nat – Billy wanted to run,
he didn't want Nat to know what he'd done.
But Hugo stepped in, he grabbed a big coat
and threw it right over his friend Billy Goat.

'Why are you all covered up?' asked Nat.
'He's cold,' said Hugo – Nat soon fixed that.
'Come sit by the stove and get warm,' she said,
'and soon you can eat my freshly baked bread.'

So rumbling, grumbling under a coat
sat a bloated and ever so hot little goat.
But worse was the feeling growing inside
of the secret which Billy was struggling to hide.

RUMBLE

GRUMBLE

GURGLE

'I'm not cold, I'm **HOT**,' blurted out Billy Goat, 'and I've got a big tummy beneath this coat.

I swallowed a lump of your bread and soon,
my tummy swelled up like a great big balloon!
Now I feel horrible deep down inside.
I'm ever so sorry, Nat,' he cried.

'Oh, Billy,' said Nat, 'that bread was still raw.
That's why it made your tummy so sore.

It had to be baked and the mix had to rise.
That's when it blows up to double the size.'

She took out the loaf and it smelled so good,
just like a freshly baked loaf really should.

'But there's no juice,' said Billy, 'and the loaf is too small.
It's my fault there isn't enough for us all.'

But Nat said, 'That's why I popped out before.
I bought us some muffins and juice from the store.'

They all sat down with a knife and a plate
and this time nobody needed to wait.
They ate muffins and jam and butter all spread,
on Nat's crusty, crumbly homemade bread.

They swallowed and slurped it all down and by then
Billy Goat's tummy was happy again.
When the breakfast was finished Nat made up a song
and both of her friends started singing along.

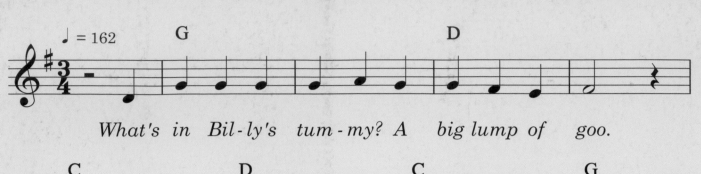

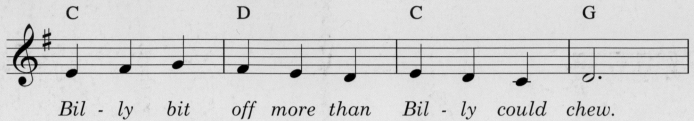

What's in Bil - ly's tum - my? A big lump of goo.

Bil - ly bit off more than Bil - ly could chew.

He thought it was bread but in - stead it was dough and

in - side his tum - my it star - ted to grow.

Oh no! Sil - ly Bil - ly, you made a mis - take. Be -

fore you can eat it the dough has to bake. So

if you don't want a bal - loon in your tum...

Next time just wait___ for Hu - go to come.

They'd eaten the food and drank the juice dry
and now it was time to be saying goodbye.
With so much fun to share between three
what a splendid big breakfast it turned out to be.